W9-BBS-419

# Baxter and Danny Stand Up to Bullying

by James M. Foley, DEd

illustrated by
Shirley Ng-Benitez

Magination Press • Washington, DC • American Psychological Association

To Beth, whose song always made us happy — *JMF*

To those who've felt even just a little bit bullied, may you
find strength in your beautiful voice and heart — *SN-B*

Published by
MAGINATION PRESS®
American Psychological Association
750 First Street NE
Washington, DC  20002

Magination Press is a registered trademark of the American Psychological Association.

For more information about our books, including a complete catalog, please write to us,
call 1-800-374-2721, or visit our website at www.apa.org/pubs/magination.

Book design by Gwen Grafft

Printed by Lake Book Manufacturing, Inc., Melrose Park, IL

Library of Congress Cataloging-in-Publication Data

Names: Foley, James M., 1947– author. | Ng-Benitez, Shirley, illustrator.
Title: Baxter and Danny stand up to bullying / by James M. Foley, DEd ;
    illustrated by Shirley Ng-Benitez.
Description: Washington, DC : Magination Press, American Psychological
    Association, [2018] | Summary: Buford Blue Jay's bullying drives Baxter
    and Danny to an open field, where they meet Queen Beth of the Bees who
    calms them and guides them in helping their friends.
Identifiers: LCCN 2017023274 | ISBN 9781433828188 (hardcover) |
    ISBN 1433828189 (hardcover)
Subjects: | CYAC: Bullying—Fiction. | Blue jay—Fiction. | Bees—Fiction. |
    Forest animals—Fiction.
Classification: LCC PZ7.1.F65 Bas 2018 | DDC [E]—dc23 LC record
available at https://lccn.loc.gov/2017023274

T 121307

Manufactured in the United States of America
10 9 8 7 6 5 4 3 2 1

Baxter the Bunny was the fastest animal in the forest. Danny the Bear was the best dancer. They would often dance and run together as they listened to the musical sounds of the stream and the wind in the trees.

One day, they heard a loud noise coming from
the trees ahead. On top of a tree sat a huge blue jay
surrounded by all of the forest jays. They were screeching.
Baxter and Danny had never heard the jays make such noise.

Baxter said, "Who are you?
Please be more quiet.
My ears are beginning to hurt."

"I am Buford Blue Jay, and I am big, blue, and beauuuutifullll! I just arrived in the forest. Thought I'd teach these little pipsqueaks how to make some real noise." Buford turned to the other jays and whispered, "Let's have some fun, boys!"

"*Screech*, *screech*, Baxter Big Ears, slow as the turtles.
Danny Boy, dopey dancer, dopey dancer...*screech*, *screech!*"

As time went by Buford and
the jays cried louder and louder.
Buford made up mean names
for all the forest animals.
The jays would cry along and
laugh and laugh.

"Slimy Snake, Slimy Snake,
*screech, screech!*
Bucktooth Beaver, Bucktooth Beaver,
*screech, screech!*"

Soon the forest was filled with the sound of jays
and the shouts of angry animals.

Baxter was angry about Buford's name-calling. Danny was sad
because he thought that he was a great dancer, not a "dopey dancer."

Baxter and Danny left the forest and ran
to the open field near Mr. Bear's garden.

Soon, they noticed
a humming sound.
It was coming from
a nearby beehive.
The gentle humming
made them feel good.

Baxter said, "Hello in there!"

Out buzzed the queen bee. "Hello," said she,
"I'm Queen Beth of the Bees. Can I beee…of help?"

"Queen Beth, your bees are so calm.
How do you keep the hive happy?"

"Staying happy is not always easy! We bees try
to say nice things to each other, stay busy
making honey, and stick together as friends.

I like to sing this song to keep us all buzzing along!

*I am great and so are you!*
*Together we can make it through.*
*Working hard, helping out:*
*That's what bees are all about!"*

Baxter and Danny began to sing along
with Queen Beth. The more they sang,
the better they felt. "Thank you, Queen Beth,
for making us happy again!"

"Why were you sad, my friends?"

"Buford Blue Jay called me 'slow as the turtles'
and Danny 'dopey dancer.'"

"Well I'll beeeee! Buford is acting like a bully.
Here's the buzz on standing up to bullying.

Stand up strong and tall.
Stick together as friends and
sing your song loud and clear.

Don't forget I'll be around if you need help!"

Baxter and Danny ran back into the forest and
stopped beside Billy Beaver's lodge. Billy looked very sad.

"Buford and the blue jays made fun of my teeth.
Now all the animals are calling me Billy Bucktooth."

Baxter and Danny said, "Billy, we are here
to help you feel better. Sing along with us.

*I am great and so are you!*
*Together we can make it through.*
*Working hard, helping out:*
*That's what we are all about!"*

"Wow, I am feeling happy again. Maybe we can help Sammy Snake. Everyone is calling him Slimy Snake because of Buford and the jays."

Soon Baxter and Danny were moving through the forest and singing their "feel good" song to all the animals who had been bullied.

All the animals
gathered around
Baxter and Danny.

Billy stepped up and said, "Thanks for making us
feel good! Come by the lodge any time for dinner!"

Baxter shouted, "Our work is not done! We have to stop the
jays from acting like bullies and face up to Buford Blue Jay."

hmmm

la
la
la!

Baxter and Danny started to sing.
The other animals joined in,
and together they walked through
the forest to Buford's tree.

Buford and the jays cried and
screeched as loud as they could.
The animals just sang their song louder.

Into the forest swarmed Queen Beth
and her bees. The forest was filled
with the sound of humming and song.

Then, a very strange thing happened. Buford stopped
puffing out his chest and flew to a nearby tree.
The other jays just looked at him and flew away.

"You were right, Queen Beth, we stuck together, sang
our song loud and strong, and Buford lost his power."

Queen Beth flew over to Buford's tree and started to hum. The bees and the animals followed her. All the animals started to sing:

*"I am great and so are you!*
*Together we can make it through.*
*Working hard, helping out:*
*That's what we are all about!"*

Buford raised his head and listened to the song. From that day on, Buford never called the animals names again!

# NOTE TO PARENTS AND OTHER CAREGIVERS

Bullying prevention programs have been in existence for over ten years in schools and youth organizations. Despite their existence, many children and adolescents continue to experience bullying. Statistics indicate that one in four students has experienced some form of bullying.

Bullying is defined as aggressive behavior that occurs repeatedly over time, is intended to cause harm, and involves an imbalance of power between perpetrator and victim. Bullying can take the form of physical, verbal, and social harassment. Cyberbullying, which involves the use of electronic communication (e.g., text messages or social media posts) can intensify the negative impact of threats, false rumors, and verbal and physical aggression.

The key to coping with bullying behavior is to help your child build self-esteem and resilience. *Baxter and Danny Stand Up to Bullying* is intended as a primer in coping with bullying presented in story form. In the story, Baxter and Danny demonstrate strategies such as reinforcing the forest animals' self-esteem, sticking together, and assertively taking action against Buford Blue Jay's bullying behavior.

## HOW THIS BOOK CAN HELP YOUR CHILD

Positive psychology research has consistently found that the underpinnings of a positive self-esteem and happiness are:

- having a positive relationship with important people in one's life, and

- being engaged in productive life activities.

In *Baxter and Danny Stand Up to Bullying*, Queen Beth's song, which keeps her hive happy, is based on those principles.

*I am great and so are you! (positive affirmation)*

*Together we can make it through. (positive relationship)*

*Working hard, helping out: (productive life activity)*

*That's what we are all about!*

The song becomes a mantra which is repeated by the forest animals and increases their feeling of self-worth. Joining together as a group empowers them to confront Buford's behavior, which restores harmony to the forest.

Reading together with your child is often a relaxed and comfortable ritual. It can be a time and space in which your child feels safe and most connected to you. This time of safe connection can be the time to begin discussion of the difficult topic of bullying. Let your child set the pace of the conversation. Listening to your child's experiences with bullying is the starting place for support and change.

## HOW TO HELP YOUR CHILD STAND UP TO BULLYING

The following are steps you can take to help your child build positive self-esteem and resilience, so they can better cope with any bullying they may face in the school years.

**Identify bullying behavior.** When reading the book with your child, use the story to highlight Buford Blue Jay's bullying behavior: name calling ("slow as the turtles," "dopey dancer") and enlisting the group of blue jays to make the individual animal feel bad. Help your child understand the effect mean words have on the other animals in the story by pointing out "Name calling makes the animals feel bad." Identifying and labeling problem behavior is important. Label this behavior "name calling," and indicate that it is unacceptable; for example, you might say something like, "You know that in our family, we want to be kind and use nice words, not call each other names!"

**Teach assertiveness at home.** When you observe "name calling" within the family, try to take the time to redirect and give a positive alternative statement. The family is a practice ground for life skills needed to stand up to bullies. Teaching assertiveness within the family can help. ("Nobody likes it when you use mean names.")

**Listen and problem solve.** Within the safe space of reading time, ask specifically about your child's concerns about bullying. Initially, keep your responses neutral in order to clarify your child's concerns. (E.g., "Have you ever seen bullying at your school?" "How often does that happen?" "How did it make you feel?") If your child is developmentally ready, involve them in the problem-solving process ("What do you think would help?" "What would stop the bullying?" "If you saw bullying, who is a good person to tell?"). Parents should give specific instructions on how to solve the situation: "I'd want you to tell me and your teacher." Children benefit from physical demonstrations and integrating lessons into their play. Use your child's favorite stuffed animals to augment your discussion. When teaching strategies, first model with the stuffed animals, then have your child use the

toys to demonstrate their understanding of the concept.

**Brainstorm coping strategies.** Use the story to illustrate the impact of Queen Beth's song, which emphasizes the forest animals' own strengths and the power of the group to stop bullying behavior. Then tell your child that they can effect change: "In this story, the song reminds the animals of their strengths, and that they have good friends. What are your strengths? Who can you rely on to be a good friend? These are the things that can help you feel better."

**Talk about social support.** Using social support is a good way to cope with stress like bullying. Point out to your child how, in the story, the animals stuck together and helped each other. Guide your child through a discussion of the positive power of their groups. For example, you could ask your child, "How does it feel when your team cheers for you or you cheer for a friend? How does it feel when the kids in school work together and have fun or make something?"

**Build self-esteem.** Your child needs a basic foundation of positive self-worth in order to stand up to future bullying. Point out on a regular basis all the wonderful qualities your child possesses and good habits they have learned. Make sure you describe your child's abilities accurately. Encourage your child by giving accurate support rather than unwarranted praise. Encouraging your child by describing their positive actions helps them develop a true sense of self-worth. Make a specific list, including qualities such as being helpful by doing chores like feeding a pet, or being kind by caring for a sibling. Take pictures of your child demonstrating those qualities. Create an electronic or actual poster containing pictures or phrases of the qualities.

**Use positive affirmations.** Help your child convert the personal qualities into a positive affirmation which can serve as a daily reminder of self worth. (E.g., "I am a great helper because I feed the dog.") Add the repeating or singing of positive affirmations to your daily routine. Begin by modeling your own positive affirmations for your child.

**Emphasize telling an adult.** Point out that Baxter and Danny relied on Queen Beth because they trusted her. Help your child identify the adults in their life whom they trust, such as family members and teachers. Make a list of those adults with your child. Discuss scenarios in which bullying may occur, and stress seeking out the trusted adult in such situations, especially when the situation feels unsafe, or when insults or teasing are persistent. Remind your child that it is a sign of strength to ask for help.

It is only natural for a parent to be worried about their child's well-being when they move into the greater world of daycare or school. Bullying is often on a parent's list of concerns. Hopefully, working on these strategies at an early age will provide a sense of control and harmony for parent and child. If you suspect that bullying is occurring, cooperating with preschool, daycare, or school professionals is essential. If problems persist, consult a qualified mental health professional.

## About the Author

**James M. Foley, DEd,** is a licensed psychologist who has recently retired from his private practice in Maine. He has served as a clinical director and member of a community mental health center children's service team and has extensive experience as a school psychologist and child and family therapist. He now resides in Sonoma County, CA, in close proximity to his two adult children, and serves as psychological consultant to a local school district. Dr. Foley can be reached at jim@therapeuticstorytime.com.

## About the Illustrator

**Shirley Ng-Benitez** loves to draw! Nature, family, and fond memories of her youth inspire her mixed media illustrations. Since '98, she's owned gabbyandco.com, designing, illustrating, and lettering for the technology, greeting card, medical, toy, and publishing industries. Currently, she's living her dream, illustrating and writing picture books in San Martin, CA, with her husband, two daughters, and pup, Zsófi. Shirley is honored to have illustrated this book as well as *Danny and the Blue Cloud* and *Baxter Turns Down His Buzz*, by Dr. James Foley, published by Magination Press. You can find more of her work on her website, www.shirleyngbenitez.com.

## About Magination Press

**Magination Press** is an imprint of the American Psychological Association, the largest scientific and professional organization representing psychologists in the United States and the largest association of psychologists worldwide.